JOURNEY TO SHAMBALA

MICHAEL ROMANO

Journey to Shambala

ISBN: 9798848405101

JOURNEY TO SHAMBALA

INTRODUCTION

The
Legendary City
Of
"Shambahala"

From the Journal and Memory of
Michael Richard John Romano
To Us, his Grand Children
In Hopes We Would Entertain Adventure
in Our Lives.
Read by Henry Robert,
Fourth of Ten

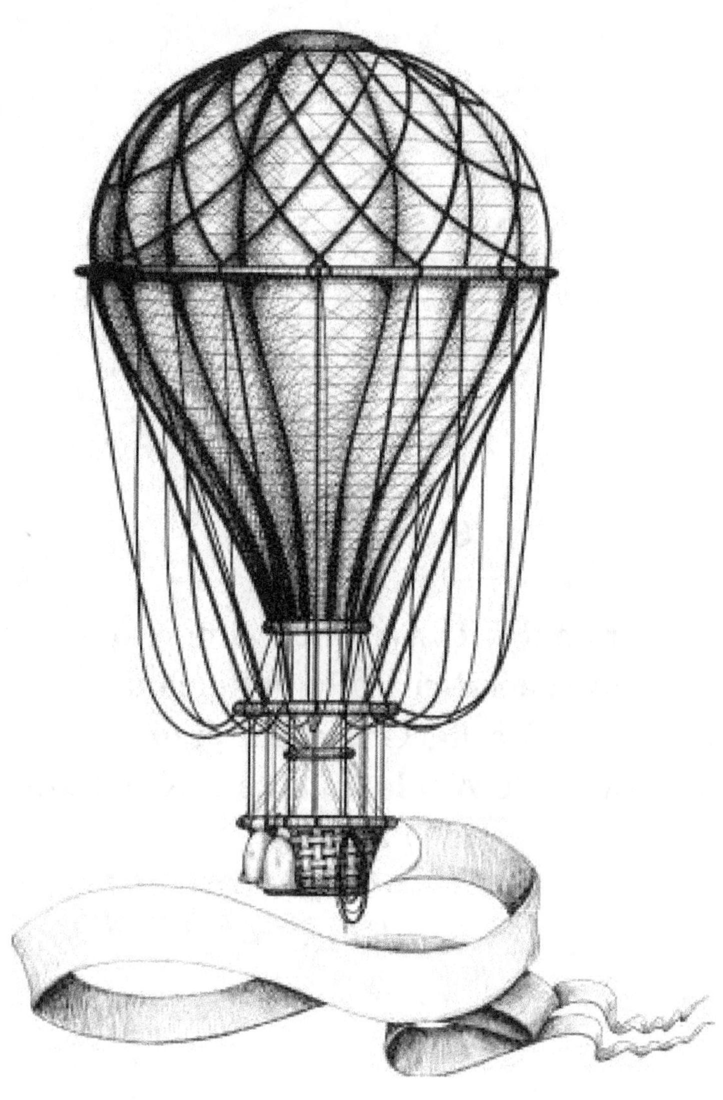

    SHAMBALA

CHAPTER ONE
SUCH A FUN BEGINNING

As a youth, the circus held almost a magical sway over thoughts in my every waking moment. From mucking the elephant stalls (Cleaning out poopie hay) to feeding chunks of meat to the not so friendly big cats; I had done every low, menial job they had to throw at me.

Summers end is near, and I am re assessing my future in the Big Top. One day, the balloonist, whom I helped rope off, fill up and set the weighted sand bags just so, started his evening drinking, just a bit too close to noon. Our ring master calling the attention of the crowd to the outside ring, in which this supremely colorful and huge balloon stood, tied to the earth by four brightly braided ropes.

Shouting again for the Master Balloonist, with no response, he got quite antsy. Then looking around, when his eyes fell on me, they sparkled.

Knowing in his heart that the pilot was consumed in his drink, quickly, and quietly, clothed me in the coat and hat of one who knew all about flying the gigantic airbag of heat. Looking around, he asked, "You do know how it works, don't you?"

Shaking my head, to what I think was an affirmative, helped me, well…more like lifted and flipped me into the basket then stood upright shouting to the audience… "This fearless soul will travel the clouds up into the heavens, only to return with wondrous tales of angels and …ahhh, the such. Release the Ropes!!!"

And *this* they did, very aptly. Only, without me being there to tell them *not* to completely let go, higher and higher I flew. Until, I was, and they were well out of sight.

Reeling in the ropes and sitting down to eat some of the food I'd hide in the box onboard for sneaking a peaceful lunch, I simply had to wait till I touched down on the ground again. Yep…that was all it would take,

I surely did hope.

<u>END CHAPTER ONE</u>
FIRST DAY OF HOW MANY
I WOULD SOON FIND OUT

CHAPTER TWO
MY ... AREN'T THE CLOUDS WIDE!

I'm glad I packed a great lunch, but better eat in small snacks. Don't know how long I'm gonna be floating up here! The day quickly sped into darkness, and stars lit the sky as I had never seen them before.

Another day and night passed, with no land either below or out front of me in sight. My decision to split up my food has given me over half left, although I think I had better make the portions smaller, from the looks of the monstrous billowy clouds, for as far as the eye can see, it seems as it may be a long, long trip.

Now day three and still nothing in sight, but it is getting even colder than it was before.

The blankets for the passengers to cuddle with on their ascensions certainly came in handy warding off frost bite!

The night of the fourth day is upon me, and vittles are getting down to scraps and crumbs.

Not a wine drinker, but the bottle the balloonist kept hidden behind the gear pile, may come in handy when my water runs out, or it gets any colder.

"WAIT," there are what seem to be some white peaks ahead.

Oh, Wow, it's starting to snow, and I'm losing altitude!

Now what? Where can I be in a land of snow capped mountains, Alaska…no, was too long for there.

Can't think where I can possibly be, except at the top of the world where it's this cold and snowy.

The almost "Ice" in the air is making for the balloon to decrease in size, dropping me lower and lower.

Now, low enough to see some rock outcroppings poking through, then snowy blanket.

Not yet close to the ground to try and land, but worried about what is below…and where the heck I was!

It seemed to get even colder as ice began forming on the visible edged of the bag.

Then…it happened! With an almost silent bang, the balloon burst, dropping me and the basket towards the ground at an angle.

This slant, allowed for me to slide over a mildly down sloped area, like my winter toboggan, coming to a halt, by what seemed to be a large pole with this symbol on it.

शम्बाला

Wasn't time to figure anything out, as I was close to being frozen solid.

Wrapping up in the blankets, grabbing the gas tank for the balloons fire, I lit it with the sparker in the tool bag, using the basket on its side for some makeshift protection from the elements.

Lord knows that the flame into the basket, along with the blankets kept me alive till morning's light was fully allowing me to assess the situation.

This came none too soon!

Well, lights out, looking around, surmising… "Yep … I'm in deeeeep trouble!"

<u>END CHAPTER TWO</u>
OUT OF THE FRYING PAN,
INTO THE, WELL…
DEEP FREEZE!

CHAPTER THREE
IS _THIS_ THE NORTH POLE?

With full sun, well, as bright as it could be through a light snow flurry, and I don't think my gas reserves will be lasting very long, I looked around for any kind of better protection from the elements.

My Dad always said I was an optimist, and I have a good feeling about my chances of getting through this. Even though a piece of my frozen hair just broke off onto then newly fallen snow I was knee deep in. In the white out, which was the visibility in every direction, somehow, I made out a dark crack in the distance.

Lumbering through the deepening snow, I reached what seemed to be a thin split in the rock faced wall. Squeezing past its sharp pointed edges, I was able to wiggle into this cave….and "What" a cave! Once in, the winds were nonexistent & temperatures were much higher. The farther I walked into it; the very nature of the place seemed "Not" to fit where I was!

There were strange symbols are carved all over the cave walls.

ट्ऋओऊघ्ःथसि पस्सगे ळीएष् थे पथ

(THROUGH THIS WAY LIES THE PATH)

Although didn't have a clue to this meaning then. I had never seen anything like this before, but so tired, can't explore right just now.

Looking further, I could see a light coming from around a distant bend in the cave's wall." Got to look into this," I said bravely to myself. Well, as brave as I could muster.

After ten minutes of climbing over pointed rocks, my weary self, seemed to tell me, really force me to plop down in order to recharge whatever energy still remained in my body's batteries.

Slipping the last crumbs of stale bread and water into myself, guess I fell off to sleep.

In a dream, could have sworn I heard voices speaking to me...and a warm soft hand on my forehead.

One eye forced its way open and a hand...oh, mine brushed over something warm and soft covering me.

Now, shaking off the wear and tear of the preceding fight with the air and nature, sat up finding myself in a darkened room, lit by an orange candle on its far side.

I was dressed in a gown of most beautiful, soft and flowing design, to my complete confusion.

At my bed's side were three pairs of footwear... slippers, shoes and taller furry boots.

I opted for the boots in case I needed to make a hasty escape!

Then, there were the giggling sounds of children from the other side of the door. Didn't sound too ominous, so I opened and looked at half a dozen youngsters playing with the deflated balloon piled in the middle of the room.

"Hey kids…where am I?"

Then off they scooted through doors in then walls I couldn't even see. But, the big one at the end of the room began to open slowly. This amazingly dressed, slight little man approached. All festooned (fancily dressed) in silks and stuff I didn't even recognize.

"My name is Asham…and yours is?"

"Uhhh, Michael Richard Romano."

"And just how did you happen to be in this locale, Michael?"

Looking around, seeing half a dozen pair of kiddie eyes squinting from behind everything, I sat down.

"Well, Asham, it's like this." Then, into my travels I deeply went, all the way to the awakening in the furry bed.

He nodded and excused himself just like that, leaving me alone, except for the giggling little monkeys hiding behind all the furniture.

Getting my bearings, decided to wave some of the young'uns out of their hiding.

With a gesture of my arm, more than I thought surrounded me. Had to be thirty of them, so I asked them to sit in a circle around me on the floor.

"Let's see...what kind of story shall I start with," I asked myself aloud.

Jack and the Beanstalk has always been a favorite. So, into it I went, mesmerizing the crowd.

At the stories end, Asham walked back into the room, this time with a deep smile on his face.

"You will do well, Michael Romano."

He then beckoned the children to leave, with a hand gesture for me to follow him. Now, what could be in store for me now?

<u>END CHAPTER THREE</u>
WHAT WONDERS TO BEHOLD

CHAPTER FOUR
THEY SAY SEEING IS BELIEVING WELL…I SEE, YET, CANNOT BELIEVE!

My benefactor led me down this ornately carved hall way to balcony, opening out to a great and opening canyon of flowers, trees, waterfalls spewing into bubbling lakes. People all around, working & singing as if not a care in them.

Where the heck was I?!

"Ahhh, my son…by the look on your face, I can surmise the question you are about to ask. Where are you?"

He smiled, slowly waving his arm out and over it all saying only one word… "Shambala."

My mind clenched for a moment trying to remember way back in my Sunday school classes for memory of that word.

"Isn't that the place where goodness and peace are supposed to repose," I think I mumbled out.

"Yes, my son, your memory has served you well."

"I had believed it was just a fairy tale to give to us kids in order to shut us up!"

Leaning over and whispering in my ear, "Apparently not," with a bit of a chuckle.

"Why, how…Why have I been brought here?"

"Well, my son, you weren't exactly *brought* here. You just kind of floated on in, as it were. As you can see, we are not exactly on the Beaten Path area for tourists."

Shaking my head, still a bit stuffy from the freezing trek, agreed.

"When you feel up to it, I'll have a guide take you about the land, showing you our wonders, does that meet with your approval?"

"Oh yes sir," I answered. And as he waived his hand, stairs appeared from the edge of the balcony, as if they suddenly grew there.

As we descended the staircase, children gathered at the bottom, followed by scores of older people, all waiting to see… Me, I guess.

As I looked at their smiling faces, the children seemed to rise to meet me.

"They're floating…

THEY'RE FLOATING!!!"

I almost shouted to Asham, as all he did was that half smile of his, nodding, saying, "All in due time."

As we walked, orchards of many kinds of fruits, recognizable to me, were on both sides of the cobbled path…yet some bore no resemblance at all to what I knew.

As were the vegetables. Most I could make out, but grown in different fashions and seriously larger.

Tomatoes the size of cantaloupes hung from vines thrice my height. The carrots some were pulling from the ground were the size of a baseball bat.

All things here were, well, just *more*! A ball bounced up front of me and I picked it up. "Throw it here, please," a youth asked.

Picking it up almost wrenched my arm out of socket. Finally getting it up, asked the closing person, "How much does this weigh?"

"Oh, I didn't know you were not from here… please allow me." Taking it, gave a heave, sending it fifty yards!

I looked back to Asham, saying, "I do need to learn more, sir, before I go much farther."

This got a full smile as he led a young lady by the hand, who was standing behind him in his shadows. I couldn't speak when she introduced herself. My goodness, what a beauty. Standing there smiling, while I simply liked like a drooling ape.

"Hi…I'm, ahh, umm…"

Thank goodness Ashram saw my lack of composure, saying, "Jo, may I introduce Mr. Michael Richard Romano, a visitor to our land."

She took my hand and kissed it. Almost fainted from the blood rushing to my head!

"Well…," Asham said, "perhaps we can meet for midday meal, after Jo has shown you the grounds, and answering some of your questions.

Shaking my head, making sure none of the spittle flung off, took her hand, then off we went.

END CHAPTER FOUR
I JUST CAN'T WAIT!

CHAPTER FIVE
WELL…THIS ISN'T
KANSAS, I CAN SAY

"Since the dawn of beings, we have been here, in order to ensure our species. Entrusted to keep and maintain just the best of human qualities. Only here, to make possible the further grace that was once given to humankind, but lost. You will be shown all our wonders by our young lady. Please feel free to ask whatever questions you may come up with, or any ideas that could improve on our ways. Please go now, you both and discover together."

Looking back at Miss Jo, I smiled and nodded…then off we went.

As we moved through the orchards of the largest most amazingly smelling fruits of every kind, there, ahead, it opened up to this large lake with six, no *seven* waterfalls cascading down into it.

People in reed fishing boats throwing nets, bringing in copious amounts of fish seemed to be singing through their tasks.

Looking at her, puzzled, she answered as is reading my mind,

"We all choose the job that makes up happy; therefore singing is only natural."

All I could do was smile and nod, as we walked on. After quite a while of silent walking, just walking through the most amazing surrounding of flowers, fruit groves, fields of any kind of edible imaginable...even the sheep looked brushed and combed, we came to these trees with a fruit completely unknown to me.

"What are these called," cupping this oddly shaped, almost cone like yellow fruit, whose smell almost made me have visions!

"Oh," she started to say, then paused. "This has no single name. Please try one." Plucking one she pointed to, I took a big and very juicy bite. My whole body shook, instantly.

Not a bad, but remarkable uplifting almost salubrious feeling of great strength.

Wide eyed, I looked back at her as I could see the wide smile upon her face. "Take another," She almost giggled.

As a ravenous beast on a piece of meat, I slurped the rest of the semi solid, but so juicy liquid…well, "No Name" fruit, then dropped to my seat on a close rock, aided by new friend.

"Just a moment and your senses will be about you again." Seemed like more than a moment before I could gather my equilibrium and, well, yes…my senses, but I felt, wonderful!

"I cannot imagine what just happened, but I will not complain of this wonderful feeling that is coming all over me."

"Jo…?"

"There is much to learn, and this is the first. Our fruit of life, it gives us longer life span, great health and strength not only of body but mind."

With saying that, she leapt from the ground we stood upon, to a rock near us, thirty feet up in the air!

"That's the physical part."

<u>END CHAPTER FIVE</u>
COULDN'T SPEAK,
JUST SHAKING MY HEAD IN WONDER

CHAPTER SIX
TO THEM, GOLD IS JUST ANOTHER COLOR

After recovering from the magical mystical fruit, getting my legs under me, decided to go on with more of the wandering tour. Pointing to a tall outcropping of stone wall, gasped at what lay before me, and quarter of a mile in each direction!

"Jo…JO…!" "Do you know what that, this, all this stuff in the wall is?!"

"It's gold. We use it for cooking, wires to transfer electrical power, and is a great reflector for diverting the sun's rays into areas of constant shade…why?"

I stopped and looked at her. She had "No" idea what its value was beyond true practical applications. What a clean, pure mind she has, not to be drawn into greed and avarice by the sight of such an amazing bounty of wealth.

"In my world, men…and women will step over each other's bleeding and dying bodies to grab any amount of this golden metal."

Her only word was, "Why?"

Thinking, I had no great answer EXCEPT, "When people get afraid of not having something, they strike out at those who have … and gold is a great big Have!"

With a look of more understanding than I would have thought she'd have, half smiled, slowly shaking her head. I nodded telling her, without words, that she was correct.

It seemed that inventive advancements were scattered everywhere as many petals in a great wind. "Look here," she asked, as waving her arm across this fully flowered tree. Suddenly, untold thousands of butterflies sprang from the branches engulfing us momentarily, then landing ever so gently all over her, then me.

"Don't touch, for danger of injury to them. Simply enjoy the communing."

What was she talking, "Commnu… "WOW," I can feel them talking, sort of, to me…all over!!! Guess I started to giggle out loud, as Jo looked over to me & began doing the same.

"Nature is one with us. This is why we need to protect Nature."

Her butterflies flew away, but mine stayed to my uneasiness.

"What…What…?"

"Oh, they are simply imparting more of their wonder," I then looked at her, "yes wonder, into you."

With a large sigh, they fluttered off, leaving me with this, for lack of a better answer, open minded appreciation of everything around me.

"See," she said, "Wonder!"

Looking at my arms, which were still glittering with a warm glow, turned to her, with my smile and slow shaking of my head, gave her to know I "Now" understood. A whole new feeling and acceptance rolled over me like a wave. Our walk became a five mile wander, although, I didn't tire at all.

Looking a bit confused, she answered without even asking … "It was the fruit. It gives you a lift of Life Energy you may never have had before."

"You have to teach me *that!*"

I got was a smile as she waved me on.

END CHAPTER SIX
SO MUCH, SO FAST

CHAPTER SEVEN
NOW IT'S COMING REALLY QUICKLY!

Taking a break, sitting on these amazingly carved boulders, she asked me if I'd like a snack.

Never have refused food before, so a quick nod ended up with a piece of fruit from that very same tree before.

"Is this ...?"

"Yes," she said as I took a big bite.

This time, as I slurped my way through the juicy sweet, my head felt as if it were tightening. Uneasily, I stopped eating and looked at her.

"Don't have any fear. You are becoming one of us, through the transformation you are feeling now."

As I was able to get many words out, asked "ONE of Us?"

"When you arrived, one of our people, a kind of a doctor, sensed you had a blood malady."

"My father died of a blood malady, but how could you possibly know? No signs of the illness have ever shown in me."

With a tilt in her nod said, "She just knows by your aura and believe it or not, your smell."

"I smell?!"

She laughed shaking her head. "It's just something she can sense. But now, you no longer have any worries of that, or really anything else you had."

Didn't think my eyes would shut again, after they popped from her answer, but strangely enough, my limbs, muscles and yes, even my mind seems to be better than it was before I bit the fruit!

At that very moment came a resounding clamor of bells, seemingly from everywhere.

People were running toward the main building from everywhere so we got into gear and joined.

"Look!"

"Over the mountain, two floating round things with flames shooting underneath," was being yelled.

As cleared the trees, I could see two balloons, as was mine, only larger, coming through the snow, down into the valley. Visible, were three people in each one.

What could this possibly mean? Was it accidental? Or did they follow to save me and get caught up in the same problems as did I?

We'd soon find out, as they descended onto the grassy area just down from the lake.

END CHAPTER NINE
SOMEHOW, I DON'T HAVE
AN EASY FEELING

CHAPTER TEN
GREED FOLLOWED

The population rallied around the balloons, amazed at this new flying machine that breathes fire. Out poured ten men and a woman.

She, by her voice, seemed to control the others. Marching up to long steps, military style, followed by her armed soldiers, stopped in front of Asham, recognizing him as leader. His stature, well over six foot in height, gave him the aire of one in charge.

"I am Elizabeth, and have come to trade with your kingdom. Having heard of a mystical place, respite with many things, we come bearing good wishes, seeing what you have to offer in exchange."

I leaned toward Jo and whispered, "They were tot coming to search for me." Thinking to myself, I guess aloud, how pompous my thinking that they would care of the well being of a nobody like me.

Where she leaned into me saying, "You are *not* a nobody!"

OOOhh, didn't know she felt that way.

"What have you brought with you, aside from those firearms of a new and visually improved state," Asham asked much more politely than would have I.

"These are to protect us against any evil we may encounter," was her snipped response.

"As you can see, here there is no evil here…well as yet," Asham answered. Her hand went down onto the handle of her pistol, as nearly a hundred citizens with bows appeared from almost thin air with arrows pointed directly at them.

"You will have no need for weapons in Shambala, please remove them to be returned on your trip home."

Although pretty angry, she wasn't foolish, ordering her people to give up their firearms immediately.

"Thank you for your display of trust," Asham said with a bit of smile in his voice.

"Now, Elizabeth…what is it you have come to trade for?"

"The yellow metal you pay your Sherpas with for the items they deliver here several times a year."

"Ahh, the yellow iron, they call Gold, is that it? And what do you offer in trade?"

Elizabeth stood erect like an officer saying, "Please bring one of the handguns to me."

Doing so carefully, and with more than sufficient arrows pointed at them from a ways back, looked as she pulled back the breech loading the first bullet. Looking around, she saw a bird flying high, aimed and pulled the trigger rapidly, placing ten bullets in the air, hitting and dropping the bird.

Asham nodded, and then with a wave of his hand, one archer let loose a single arrow. The very same kind of bird, even farther away fell.

"You see, madam, we have sufficient for our needs." Yeah, this huffed her but she held her tongue, for now.

"Have you no threats here you wish to protect yourself against," she blurted out, I think more sternly than she wanted to.

"Not until today," Asham answered.

END CHAPTER TEN
AND "NOW" THE DANCE BEGINS!

CHAPTER ELEVEN
YEP… MORE DID FOLLOW

We were all invited to a grand meal at dinner time. The new visitors all sat shoulder to shoulder with their backs to the wall that had nor doors or windows.

Asham led the mealtime thankful prayer as the six sat upright as if waiting for the other shoe to drop! Although the meal was quite excellent. Not a word was said till near the meal's end.

"What do you want to trade for your yellow iron," she asked rather bluntly.

"All things we need, we either make ourselves. For the rest, our Sherpas bring in twice a year. So, you see, we have no need for what you are offering," Asham said, as he stood, beckoning them to the rooms prepared for them.

"These are your accommodations until you are ready to leave. Please tell us of any special needs," he said, then turned, leaving the room through what seemed to be a door that wasn't there.

In single line, they marched to their rooms, speaking amongst themselves.

She showed me my room. Even though the bed was quite large and had an overstuffed down feather mattress on it, sleep wasn't in the stars. Tossing and turning, footsteps of more than one person, made me edge towards the crack opening of my door.

There were the curious ones, in the main room looking in every drawer and box, until they found their weapons. This was a bad sign.

Slipping out to find either Jo or Asham, I heard the chambering of a rifle round behind my head. A sound from hunting with Dad, that one never forgets.

Then the tap, tap, tap of a rifle barrel on the back of my head.

"Walk," is all I heard, and I obeyed.

Into the main room, there was Asham, Jo and a dozen more of the guards, all strapped to their chairs.

"As you see, we are not playing the happy visiting traders anymore," their leader said. She stood high atop a table, giving her demands. You will bring us sufficient gold to fill our Airships and we shall leave. You will be unharmed, as long as no one disobeys. Then, you will never see us again!"

I knew this was a lie, as once you feed the rat, it will always return, I mumbled.

Asham slightly turned to me, smiled and nodded.

He, then, looked up at her, with a smile, saying, "This will be no problem as we can fill your order before the sun rises."

Their leader looked down at him with half-amazement, half-crazed smile for the ease of becoming insanely rich.

They untied us, allowing all to do their work, except keeping Asham, Jo and Myself hostages.

As the morning sun's beams broke over the peaks, in came running one of the previously tied up assistants with news of the completion of their task.

Carefully backing up to the balloons, always holding us under the sights of their guns, climbed into their ships and started the flamed to lift off. A strange look came over her face as the balloons didn't lift for all the gold's huge weight.

"More flame," she roared, as they began, slowly, to lift upwards. Her smile became almost, that of a crazed maniac, as she yelled, "We did it!!"

Off they went, slowly, until they cleared the ridge into the ravaged of zero temperature, huge winds and ice in the air.

I looked to Asham, about to ask how he could do all this without any seeming worries at all.

Then I saw the frost begin to appear on the balloons.

Grabbing one of the telescopes an assistant had, looked as ice formed up and up the sides, until converging at the top.

"Why didn't that happen when they came in," I asked.

"Two reasons," he said.

"One, they came from the south side and we set up their Airships on the north. Second and more important, have you any idea what all that gold must weigh? My son, we reap what we sow. The world is a better place with them sent to whichever next plane they arrive at."

Now, I understood.

The south side was less protected, so colder. The tremendous weight added to the strain on the burners already maxed out from the ice and freezing winds, from the great canyon below, was more than they could overcome to keep them aloft.

"You knew all along, didn't you?"

With a calm face, nodded, as he turned, asking his assistants to serve everyone breakfast, as he needed to go off to pray for their souls.

Following him, I saw his sanctum, with paintings of him on the walls, over many years.

Quietly reading the dates, counting on my fingers the time since the first, 1716 to the date today in 1866…

"That's 150 years. He doesn't look a day over 60," I seemed to say out loud.

A small laugh as he pulled out my seat at the table.

"Many have come here trying to strip Shambala of its riches, whether the yellow iron or the advances we have achieved. None, yet, have been stopped from leaving with their thought treasures. And none have reached their destinations."

"Seems Mother Nature and simple lack of goodness are against them," I answered. My benefactor nodded and smiled.

We sat and ate, as Asham excused himself to pray.

END CHAPTER ELEVEN
A LONG ONE
BUT STUFF STARTED TO HAPPEN!

CHAPTER TWELVE
TIME SEEMS TO FLOAT BY

Awakening with birds on my window ledge, singing to me, was a feeling like no other.

Jo would take me to the book library, teaching me things which were not yet in my world: types of machinery to lift people, deep drilling apparatus, along with pumps allowing them to pump up and down hills for great lengths with little effort.

Their crops grew so much larger and taller than any I'd ever come across. All this was taught to me, while also playing with nature, animal and especially Jo.

As I grew in knowledge, my time here seemed to pass effortlessly, until one day, Asham came to me saying,

"Is it your wish to remain here or return to your home?"

Well...this was out of nowhere, leaving me speechless. Looking him directly in the eyes, said, "I think I would like to see my home again."

"An honest answer," he said, telling me that provisions would be ready for the journey when the Sherpas came in the morning.

Stunned, I thanked him, wandered out into the gardens and sat on that same carved rock, where she and I first did.

Feeling a gentle touch on my shoulder, I turned to see Jo's sad smile. "I will miss every day I do not see your face," she whispered then went off into the woods leaving me on the rock.

Didn't sleep that night.

At the dawn's first glimmer, Asham came in telling me it was time. Clothes for the trip were brought in and a sled with things from everyone were tightly packed for the trip back. Looking around for my friend's face gave me sorrow as she was not to be seen. Not till I reached the farthest point of the cave, prior to going into the freezing winds. I turned back to see her holding up her hand.

I waved and suddenly was engulfed by a blinding snow storm, obliterating all vision in every direction. Were it not for my guides, I would have lay down and been completely lost, right then.

Six days travel in the most inclement weather on the planet, led us to arrive at their village. It was a mere three days down an easy mountain side to a place where I could go by rail to port shipping.

Then a several weeks ship trip home. But *where* was home? No longer was I sure.

END CHAPTER TWELVE
A LONG TRIP, FROM START TO NOW

CHAPTER THIRTEEN
SAME TOWN, BUT NOT QUITE THE SAME LOOK

When I arrived, all seemed a bit older, not quite as sparkling as when I left, or was yanked away from, in reality. Walking down the main street, there was my favorite store, Henry's Ice Cream Parlour.

Henry the owner was there scooping the magic frozen delight when he stopped as I walked in.

"Are you a son or even a grand son of a boy named Michael Romano?"

Looking completely baffled, said, "I AM Michael Romano."

"Yeah, Junior of somewhere down the family tree, right."

"No," I said, I am the only one I know."

"Why do you act so oddly to me?"

Taking a step back, looking well at him asked, are you Henry's Grandpa?

Now…he started to shake.

I figured it was time for me to make a hasty exit! Seeing the banners up as I traveled down the street that said "4TH OF JULY PARADE SUNDAY" 1899.

Wow, a parade.

What… 1899!!!

Looking around, noticing that no one seemed familiar. I should have recognized someone!

Then, as I stopped in front of the general store, I used to do odd chores for, noticed my reflection. Twisting one way, then another…

Hey, I'm taller! Look at my face. I'm older too!

I began walking in a bit of a frenzy, right into the middle of the folks surrounding then band stand for the beginning of the concert and plopped down on the grass behind. With my face in my hands, shaking my head in order to snap myself back into reality, I felt a soft hand on my shoulder. I looked up at a face I knew.

"Jo … how, what, WHY are you here?!"

"When you left, I knew you wouldn't be able to grasp the time passed in Shambala to home time."

"I dressed up like a Sherpa, hiding in the back of the line to see how you would take to this amazing but terrifying change."

Looking at her face, calmed me so much, all I could do was nod my head.

"Do you have a place you favor to have food that we may sit and talk?"

Thinking where, as I had nowhere to live anymore, answered, "Yes… Mr. Marino's Ice Cream Emporium!" I only hope it's still there. Rounding several corners, her hand in mine, annnndd, there it was.

"Glad some things haven't changed," leaning over I said to Jo. Sitting down in a booth near the counter, I noticed the soda jerk standing there was Mr. Marino!

"Hey Mr. Marino…been a long time, but you haven't aged a day!"

Looking at me confused, then a smile came to his lips as he spoke.

"Oh…you mean my Grandpa. Folks say I'm the spittin' image of him."

Shaking my head yes, he certainly did.

"It has been a long time Michael, and all you knew are either gone, or much, much older," she whispered.

<u>END CHAPTER THIRTEEN</u>
A RUDE AWAKENING

ICE CR
PARLO

CHAPTER FOURTEEN
THE NEW BEGINNING

Sitting outside on a big rock in the town's park near Henry's, she put something into my hand. It was a smooth leather bag with bumps out of it.

She whispered, "A gift from Asham in order to start your...*our* new life."

Much louder than I meant, said "Our Life?"

She smiled, kissed my cheek and pointed to the pouch. Pouring some of it'd contents into my hand, my eyes caught the amazing sparkle or the sun off the diamonds, rubies and emeralds!"

"Jo, Look!"

She giggled, saying I had better put them back it he bag for the moment as not to raise questions. Faster than they poured out, I had them back in.

"Oh, by the way…I put some handfuls of very old gold coins in the bottom of your back pack too. My head exploded with not only the joy of her wanting to be mine, but the riches of a king at our command.

"We need to find things worthy of these that can help and direct our fellow people, so they may be able to use Shambala's gifts when the time may come."

That was what Jo was waiting to hear from me. Her smile was from her heart, both for me and the words that came from my lips.

"Now we can start building out dynasty, of a strong and true lineage to always be proud of."

That's when I started the town's Library, Children's Hospital and the Public Kitchen for those who are hungry.

I only hope you, my children, will keep up the wonderful things your Grand Mother and I have started.

Bless and keep you all well,

Love Great Grandpa Michael
Oh, & Great Grandma Jo too!

I stopped reading Great Grandpa's memoirs and slowly turned to Granny.

Something popped in my mind as my eyes caught hers, and then she smiled.

"You're the *Jo*, aren't you? But…but…"

"You have a quick mind, like Michael had. We shall sit down after dinner and I will answer the, hmmmm, thousand questions you have," she said with that same giggle grandpa always had, as she slowly walked into the kitchen, still shaking her head, quietly laughing to herself.

Oh wow, a thousand questions won't be Nearly enough!!!"

"By the way Grandma, what about that floating thing?

With a wink, off the ground she rose …. "Yeah, THAT'S It!!!"

<u>THE END</u>

FOR NOW … TILL SHE TEACHES ME THAT FLOATING THING!